GROLIER
BOOK CLUB EDITION

Available only in the United States until January 1, 1983

Library of Congress Cataloging in Publication Data: Main entry under title: Walt Disney's The adventures of Mr. Toad. (Disney's wonderful world of reading ; 48) SUMMARY: Toad trades Toad Hall for a fast red motorcar, only to later be jailed as a car thief. [1. Animals—Fiction] I. Grahame, Kenneth, 1859–1932. Wind in the willows. II. Walt Disney. III. The Adventures of Ichabod and Mr. Toad [Motion picture] IV. Title: Adventures of Mr. Toad. V. Series. PZ7.A26194 [E] 81-2783 AACR2 ISBN: 0-394-84818-7 (trade); 0-394-94818-1 (lib. bdg.)

Manufactured in the United States of America   4   E F G H I J K

Walt Disney's
The Adventures of Mr. Toad

With characters from the Walt Disney Motion Picture
The Adventures of Ichabod & Mr. Toad

Adapted from *The Wind in the Willows*
by Kenneth Grahame

Toad was crazy about driving.
He loved a wild ride in his
gypsy cart.

Did Toad care where he was going?
Of course not!
Toad just cared about going fast
and having fun.

But Toad was a terrible driver.
He ran into things.
He ruined trees and broke fences.
Then he had to pay for them.

His friends Rat and Mole watched Toad sadly.
"Toad must give up his gypsy cart," said Rat.
"It is costing him too much money."
"But Toad swears he never will," sighed Mole.

MacBadger lived with Toad.
He took care of Toad Hall.
One day MacBadger asked Rat
and Mole to come at once.
Toad was in trouble.
His money was almost gone.

"Bills and more bills!" cried
MacBadger. "If there are any more bills,
Toad will have to sell Toad Hall!"
He threw a pile of bills into the air.
"We will help," said Rat and Mole.

Just then Toad came in the door.
MacBadger wasted no time.
He told Toad the bad news.
"Sell Toad Hall?" cried Toad. "Never!"
"Then there is only one thing to do,"
said Rat.

Rat and Mole took Toad to his room.
"You must stay here until you forget
about gypsy carts," said Rat.

To make sure that Toad did not leave,
Rat locked the door.

It was a good plan.
There was only one thing wrong with it.
It did not work.
As soon as night came, Toad sneaked
out the window.

Cyril the horse was waiting.
"Which road shall we take?" asked
Cyril. "The high road? The low road?"
"The road to adventure!" cried Toad.

And off they went—toad, horse, and
gypsy cart!

In the early morning they came
to an inn.

Parked outside was a beautiful
red motorcar.

SIGN OF THE MUG
INN

"A motorcar!" cried Toad.
He forgot all about gypsy carts.
He had to have that motorcar.

Toad walked into the inn.

There sat the Weasel Gang.

Toad did not know that the weasels
were famous car thieves.

"Who owns that red motorcar?" asked
Toad. "I want to buy it."

"It belongs to me and the Weasel Gang,"
said Mr. Winkie, the innkeeper. "How much
will you pay for it?"

Toad took out
his wallet.
It was empty.
"All I have is
this deed to my
house," said Toad.

"It's a deal!" cried Winkie.
He snatched up the deed and signed it.
Toad signed it, too.

"The motorcar is yours, Toad!"
said Winkie. "And Toad Hall
belongs to us."

Winkie and the weasels waved good-bye
to Toad.

He drove away smiling.

Poor Toad!

He did not know the truth.

The car was stolen!

By and by Toad noticed that he was
being followed—by a policeman!

Toad stopped the car.

The policeman told him, "I am taking you to jail."

"Whatever for?" asked Toad.

"For stealing this car!" said the policeman.

The next day, Toad's friends read about Toad in the newspaper.

"I knew Toad's wild ways would get him into trouble," said Rat.

"But Toad would never steal," said Mole. "It must be a mistake."

Daily Bugle

MR. TOAD ARRESTED!

CHARGED WITH CAR THEFT

"If only he had kept the gypsy cart!"
said Rat.

"If only we had locked the window!"
said MacBadger.

Toad had to go
to court.

He told his story
to the judge.

"I bought the car
from Winkie," said
Toad. "I gave him
Toad Hall for it."

Winkie told his
story next.

"I never heard of
Toad Hall," he said.

"All I know is . . .
this toad tried to
sell me a stolen car!"

No one believed Toad.
Everyone believed Winkie.
The judge sent Toad to jail.

Poor old Toad!
He was locked up
and left all alone.

Then someone came
to visit him.

Toad did not know who she was.
"Surprise!" said the visitor.
It was Cyril—in a disguise!

"I have a dress for you, too," said Cyril. "And a hat that is just your size!"

Toad put them on.

"No one will know it is you, Toad," said Cyril.

Cyril was right.
Toad walked right past the guard
and out the gate.

Hours later,
a tired Toad was
still walking in
the rain.
He was on his
way to Rat's house.

Rat and Mole were sitting in front of
a warm, cozy fire.

They were drinking cocoa.

"Life isn't much fun without Toad.
Is it, Ratty?" said Mole.

"I miss him," said Rat.

Just then they heard a knock.

Rat opened the door.

Toad fell into the room with a PLOP!

"I didn't do it," said Toad in a tired
little voice. "But no one believes me."

"I believe you!"
said MacBadger as
he came in the door.

MacBadger had amazing news.
Winkie and the Weasel Gang
were living in Toad Hall!
"That proves you told
the truth, Toady," said
MacBadger.

That night the friends got into a rowboat.
They set out for Toad Hall.
Weasels or no weasels—they would find
the deed.
They would prove that Toad was innocent.

One of the weasels was
guarding the bridge.
The friends rowed under it.
The weasel did not see them.

At last they came to Toad Hall.
They rowed through a secret tunnel.

The tunnel led to
some stairs.

The stairs led
to a door.
Ever so slowly,
they opened it.

They found themselves in a hall
above the living room.

Right below them was Winkie—
fast asleep.

And there in his jacket was
the deed!

They made a special rope
and lowered Mole with it.
Mole had to stretch really
far to reach the deed.
But he did it!

Then the four friends decided to go to the police.

The police would see Winkie's name on the deed to Toad Hall.

They would know the truth.

The next day the newspaper told all about it.

Toad was innocent!

Daily Bugle

MR. TOAD IS INNOCENT!

WEASEL g
ARREST

The police took Winkie and the weasels
to jail.

There the gang would stay for a long,
long time.

Toad Hall was safe!

A few days later, Rat, Mole, and
MacBadger were all at Toad Hall.

"Isn't it grand?" said Mole. "Toady
is back and we are all together again."

"Yes, Moley," said MacBadger. "But
the best news is—Toad has changed. He
has given up motorcars forever."

Suddenly there was a huge crash.
Bricks began falling from the roof!
Mole ran to the window.
He saw an airplane sailing past
a broken chimney.
On the plane was Toad!

The three friends rushed outside.
They stared up at Toad.
"His new love is airplanes," said
MacBadger. "He is crazy about them!"

Had Toad changed?
Of course not!
He was the same old Toad.
Full of adventure!
Full of fun!
Loveable old Toad!